Mr Putter and Tabby
Paint the Porch

Cynthia Rylant

Mr Putter and Tabby Paint the Porch

illustrated by
Arthur Howard

W

FRANKLIN WATTS
LONDON•SYDNEY

For Bill and Susan's new little painter
—C.R

To Cora Howard, who really knows how to paint a porch
—A.H.

First published in the UK in 2001 by
Franklin Watts
96 Leonard Street
London EC2A 4XD

ISBN 0 7496 4090 1 (hardback)
ISBN 0 7496 4209 2 (paperback)

UK edition copyright © 2001 by Franklin Watts

Text copyright © 2000 by Cynthia Rylant
Illustrations copyright © 2000 by Arthur Howard
Published by arrangement with Harcourt, Inc.

A CIP catalogue record for this book is available from the British Library

Printed in China

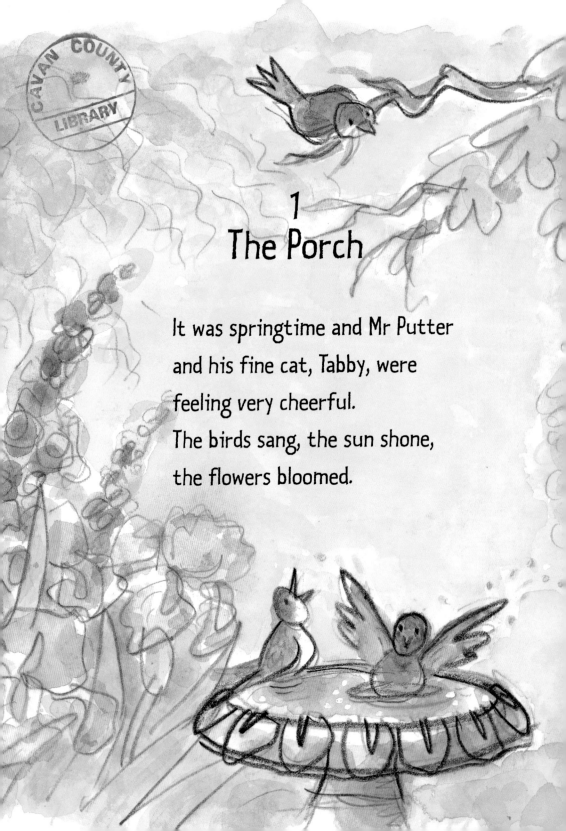

1
The Porch

It was springtime and Mr Putter
and his fine cat, Tabby, were
feeling very cheerful.
The birds sang, the sun shone,
the flowers bloomed.

Mr Putter and Tabby went out
onto the front porch with
a book.
"Let me read you a funny story,"
Mr Putter said to Tabby.
Tabby purred.
She liked funny stories.

She curled up beside Mr Putter
and waited.
And waited.
And waited.

But Mr Putter was not looking
at the book.
He was looking at a porch post.
"Hmmm," said Mr Putter.

He picked up Tabby and
looked more closely.
"Hmmm," he said again.
Mr Putter walked all around the
porch, looking and saying, "Hmmm."

Finally he said, "Tabby, this
porch needs some paint.
First I am going to paint the porch.
Then I will read you a story."
Tabby purred.
She loved Mr Putter's plans.
Especially when they included her.

She followed him to the basement,
swishing her tail,
happy it was spring.

2
Scat!

Mr Putter carried his painting
things to the porch.
He had a pot of pink paint,
a big brush,
and some rags.

Suddenly one of the rags got away.
Tabby chased it across the porch
and caught it.
"Good cat," said Mr Putter,
patting her on the head.

Tabby purred.
She might be old, but she could
still catch a wild rag when
she had to.

Mr Putter dipped his brush
into the pot and began
to paint.

As he painted, he began to sing.
He sang about paper roses and
blue bonnets and
coming around mountains.

19

Tabby purred and purred.

This was even better than a story.

Mr Putter didn't yodel

when he read a story.

All was going well when
suddenly a squirrel showed up.
The squirrel jumped onto a
freshly painted porch rail.
"Shoo!" said Mr Putter.

The squirrel jumped onto
another rail.
"Scat!" said Mr Putter.
Then the squirrel ran across
the floor of the porch.
"Scram!" said Mr Putter.

And that's when Tabby remembered
how good she was at chasing things.
"Yikes!" yelled Mr Putter.

The squirrel ran and Tabby ran.
And before it was all over,
Mr Putter's porch just sort of
painted itself.

24

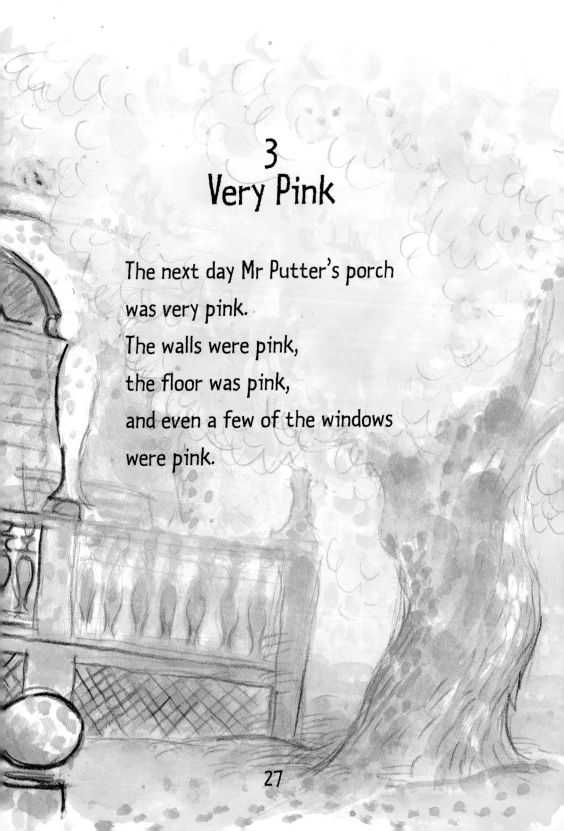

3
Very Pink

The next day Mr Putter's porch
was very pink.
The walls were pink,
the floor was pink,
and even a few of the windows
were pink.

And Tabby was *very* pink.

28

Mr Putter's neighbour
Mrs Teaberry walked over
with her good dog, Zeke.
"Oh dear," she said, looking
at Mr Putter's porch.
Zeke was sniffing Tabby's
pink whiskers.

Mr Putter sighed.

"I'll have to do it all over again,"
he said.

"Well then, we will help," said
Mrs Teaberry, rolling up her sleeves.

So Mr Putter went back to
the basement.
Tabby followed, swishing her
pink tail.

Soon Mr Putter and Mrs Teaberry
were putting blue paint over pink.

All was going well
until suddenly a chipmunk showed up.
It jumped on a rail.
It ran across the porch.

And then *Zeke* remembered how good
he was at chasing chipmunks!

4
A Lovely Yellow

The next day Tabby and Zeke stayed
inside Mrs Teaberry's house while
Mr Putter painted his porch.
Again.
He covered up all of the pink
paw prints and all of the blue
paw prints and made the porch
a lovely yellow.

When the porch was dry,
Mrs Teaberry arrived with Tabby
and Zeke.

Mr Putter was happy to have
Tabby back.

He brought a book out on the porch
and said that he would read a
funny story to everyone.

But just as Mr Putter was about
to begin, a pink squirrel and a blue
chipmunk walked by.

And Mr Putter and Mrs Teaberry laughed so hard, they didn't even *need* a funny story!

43

The illustrations in this book were done in pencil, watercolour,
gouache and Sennelier pastels on vellum paper.

Don't miss Mr Putter and Tabby's other adventures:

Mr Putter and Tabby Pour the Tea
0 7496 4087 1 (hbk)   0 7496 4206 8 (pbk)

Mr Putter and Tabby Fly the Plane
0 7496 4089 8 (hbk)   0 7496 4208 4(pbk)

Mr Putter and Tabby Walk the Dog
0 7496 4088 X (hbk)   0 7496 4207 6 (pbk)